FAITH'S FIRE

First edition. July 13, 2021.

Copyright © 2021 Sarah Amberson.

ISBN: 979-8215722848

Written by Sarah Amberson.

FAITH'S FIRE

SARAH AMBERSON

Faith looked up at the sky. The sun was shining down, making her back ache from the heat.

"Do you want to walk for a while?" Her younger sister Anna poked her head out from the back part of the wagon.

Faith hesitated. There was so much of the wagon trail that they had to take on foot out of necessity, it seemed a shame to walk when they could ride.

But then again, they had been riding all day and she was sore from sitting on the hard boards and the constant jarring.

"Okay, we can walk for a while. Will you be fine, ma?" Faith turned to her mother who was guiding the pair of oxen.

It wasn't like they needed much guiding. They sort of followed whatever was in front of them, and that was a long line of covered wagons. So many people were headed to California. Faith could hardly wait to see what was so great about it.

Most of the people going to California, at least had a man in the family. They were going to mine gold.

Faith had tried to tell her mother that women mining gold probably wouldn't be considered very proper. But her mother was adamant that there were other needs in the mining towns of California. They could wash clothes or cook or care for people's children. Or marry a man who was a gold miner and therefore still benefit from the gold everyone always seemed to be talking about.

Faith still wasn't sure exactly what they would end up doing out west. But she was ready to work hard and that was all that mattered. As long as they stuck together and pulled their weight, they would be fine.

"I can handle a couple of oxen. You girls go and stretch your legs. Anna, if you need to, stop and rest, okay?"

Faith nodded and hopped down from the wagon. It wasn't moving that fast. In fact, she was fairly certain she could walk much faster than the oxen were plodding. In a couple of hours, they were supposed to meet up with a smaller group of wagons that was headed to a specific town in California.

Faith thought back to her mother's warning. Anna had been having trouble breathing when she over exerted herself. Faith and her mother were hoping that it was just dust from all of the traveling. But Faith was worried that if Anna wasn't careful, it could get worse.

Anna was determined not to let the new challenge get her down. Slowing her down, was nearly impossible. She was an energetic girl and the only thing that slowed her down were the strange bouts of wheezing that usually happened when she ran too much.

"So, are you excited about splitting off from the main group?" Anna's voice brought her back to the present.

"No, not really. A smaller group means it will be more dangerous and probably more chances of someone attacking us. There are Indians out here, bandits, gangs, gunslingers and who knows what else." Faith shivered. She had heard enough of the stories about these trails to be afraid, no matter how many other covered wagons surrounded them.

"Do you really believe in all those stories? We have been on the wagon train for nearly three months now and I haven't seen a single Indian."

"Maybe not, but that doesn't mean they aren't out there."

"Maybe when the group is smaller, we can get to know everyone better. Maybe you will meet someone handsome who will marry you and then the two of you will be rich." A dreamy look crossed Anna's face.

"I am not really interested in wealth." Faith shrugged. "Money is nothing if you don't have love and trust and all the other things that make up a good relationship."

"Do you really believe that? What if you are poor and have nothing to eat, but love each other?"

"Well, then I suppose that would be better than having everything and hating each other." Faith hated the idea of being trapped in a marriage she couldn't stand. She had seen it before... neighbors that fought all the time and seemed to hate each other living in the same house. That would be just miserable. If she married, she wanted it to be for true, genuine love, nothing more.

The couple that had lived next to them back in the city had shouted at each other and slammed doors. It was terrible for both of them and worse for the children they had and for the family members who had to live with them.

Money could not fix any of that. But she didn't expect her fourteen-year-old sister to understand. It would be a long time until Anna would be old enough to have the opportunity to marry someone.

"Well, I think that I want a rich husband. Then I would make him love me so I could have both."

Faith giggled. That was just the sort of answer she expected from Anna. "You can't *make* someone love you. It doesn't matter how much you want someone to love you. If they don't, that is just the way it is. It just happens sometimes."

Anna shrugged. "You never know. I think that I could get most people to love me."

Faith could not dislike her sister's enthusiasm. She was very loveable and Faith was fairly certain that she would have no trouble finding a husband or someone to love her.

But she wasn't about to encourage Anna to go looking for a husband, for love, or anything else that led to marriage just yet. She was very young and still had time to prepare for all of that.

Faith on the other hand was of marrying age. At nineteen, her mother was already asking her if there was a man who had caught her eye and there was indeed not one that had even peaked her curiosity.

"Even if I am not ready to find a husband, I still think you could. We are going to be with the people from the other wagons for two more months, and they are going the same places as us, so they'll probably even live in our town." Anna's eyes lit up. "Then you can have children for me to play with."

Faith shook her head, amusement on her mind. "You are funny, Anna. But I think that is unlikely."

"You never know." Anna grinned and skipped ahead. "You never know."

—-*—-

The day seemed to stretch longer and longer. Faith took a turn guiding the oxen to give her mother a break. Then she and Anna walked some more. By the time that evening came around and it was time to meet up with their new group of traveling companions mixed with some of the old ones, Faith was relieved. She was ready for something different to happen, even if it was only temporary and then would lead to more of the same thing as before.

The transition was rather uneventful and unexciting much to both Anna's and Faith's disappointment. The wagons that were headed towards Sandy Rock, California, simply split off to another road where a small camp of covered wagons was waiting for them. Then seamlessly, the entire group kept going.

The small group of forty wagons that were going on to Sandy Rock California made Faith feel uneasy. She didn't like the idea of being so unprotected. For some reason, she had felt safer in the larger group, even if the security had probably been false. Forty compared with more than one hundred felt almost naked.

"Let's take a walk around, Faith. Let's go meet some of the new people. Maybe there will be some girls who are my age." Anna pulled at Faith's arm.

She was reluctant. She didn't really want to go and meet different people, but she knew that Anna was already missing the two girls who had become her friends from the other wagons. They had not been headed to the same town and so Anna had been forced to part ways with them.

"Fine, fine, I will come along with you, but we need to come back straight away as soon as we've gone around once, okay?" Faith figured they would walk to the front of the wagon train, to the back and then meet up with their own wagon which was around the middle.

Of course, there were way too many wagons, even in this smaller train, to stop by each and every one of them. They were going to have to settle for a majority and hope that Anna found a friend in one of them.

Anna seemed happy with her proposal and was jumping up and down with excitement.

As they went, they met other young women and some young men who were either doing the same as them, trying to explore, or simply walking for a bit of a rest from riding in their wagons.

The wagon train was slowing, and people were setting up camp. They were moving the wagons to make a wide circle. In the middle, they would keep some of the animals and they would set up their fires and their tents if they decided to sleep in them.

Some of the men and boys would sleep under the wagons while a lot of the women and children would either sleep inside the wagons or in a tent.

For Faith, Anna and their mother, they would set up a small tent with some of their blankets in front of their wagon.

The wagon was carrying way too much stuff for them to all sleep comfortably inside.

When it was pouring down rain, then they would all squeeze into the wagon and do their best to catch a few winks of sleep. But it was so cramped that one or two of them would have to sleep sitting up and that made it nearly impossible to wake up feeling rested in the morning.

Having the wagons all stopped and making camp made it easier for them to walk by and see who was in each one. Some of them were people they had already met. A pair of elderly people seeking their last adventure was one of the more familiar faces that Faith recognized; Mr. and Mrs. Campbell. They were a nice couple, full of hopes and bravery, despite their older age.

"Look!" Anna pointed over towards a covered wagon that had already set itself up for the night.

There was a fire burning on the ground and a group of children playing some sort of game.

They were around Anna's age and there were a few older people nearby that were Faith's age.

"Can we stop by? Please?" Anna asked.

"I don't know. We need to gather the firewood and get back to ma. Remember I said that we would just walk around once."

"I know, but they are right there. We can just introduce ourselves and then go back with the wood, okay?"

"Okay, I suppose that is fine." Faith felt a sudden wave of embarrassment wash over her. She wasn't sure how she felt about walking up to perfect strangers and introducing herself. She didn't like talking that much with people she knew, much less people that she didn't know.

But Anna was pulling her forward and not giving her much of a choice, so Faith allowed herself to go along.

When they got there, Anna let go of her hand and rushed up to the younger girls who seemed to be deep in conversation.

Faith stood on the sidelines, watching the girls interact. It seemed easy for Anna to find friends. It also seemed easy for the girls to accept her. In a matter of minutes, they were all chatting as if they had known each other for years.

For a moment, Faith let herself be a bit jealous. But she knew that her sister was simply different than her and there was nothing bad about that.

"Excuse me, I haven't seen you before. Did you come with the new wagons?" A deep voice interrupted her thoughts.

She looked up to find a tall young man standing there. He had a square jaw and dark hair that fell over his forehead in a sloppy, but attractive kind of way. he had dark brown eyes that seemed endlessly deep and a gentle expression on his face.

For a moment, Faith found herself speechless and didn't know what to say.

"I- I mean, yes, we are from the new wagons. My sister and I are traveling with our mother and we are going to Sandy Rock, California." Faith didn't know why she started to say everything at once. She had to stop herself and make herself wait for him to say something.

"It's good to have some new faces in our group. We've been traveling for a while now." The young man crossed his arms and took a more relaxed stance that made Faith feel a little more relaxed too. "My name is Stephan. Those girls are the daughters of a couple that I met on the way."

"I'm Faith and that is my sister Anna." Faith looked over to where Anna was still talking to her new friends.

"It's nice to meet you, Faith."

"So, are you heading to California for the gold?" Faith found herself hoping that Stephan would say that wasn't the case. For some reason, Faith thought that Stephan seemed like the type of person to have more important, ambitious aspirations.

"No. I am going out west because I want to be a preacher. I already am in a sense, I suppose. I studied under our preacher back home, even gave a few sermons in the church. But even though he wanted me to stay, I felt like my calling led me out west, to California. They need preachers out here too and I guess I was ready ofr a touch of adventure too."

Faith's heart beat a little faster. "A preacher? That's wonderful. Your family must be so proud of you." Faith had always admired the stories she'd heard of the men that risked their lives to go out west and speak with people and guide the churches for those who had none.

"They aren't, actually. My father is a banker and he was quite upset when he learned that I wouldn't be taking over the family business."

"I'm sorry. What about your mother?" Faith couldn't imagine that a mother wouldn't want her son to be a preacher. Faith could think of few things that she considered equally as brave.

"She was upset too. Risking my life, moving so far away from them, was a bit much for her but she will adjust. I know it has been hard on them, so I don't blame them for how they feel."

"I'm sorry." Faith felt sad to think of Stephen all alone, pursuing his dream. But it also made her admire him more and want to get to know more about him.

Anna's predicting words came back to taunt her. She needed to stay away from Stephen before Anna's predictions came true. She almost laughed out loud. There was no way that someone like Stephan hadn't already found a woman to share his dreams with anyway.

"It's fine. This is what I feel called to do and I am quite confident that it is the right thing for me."

Faith smiled at him, unsure what else she could say to be of further encouragement.

"We should go, my mother is probably waiting for us," Faith said suddenly. It was like she was tripping all over herself when it came to Stephen.

"Some of us get together here in the morning to pray for the days travels. You are welcome to join us tomorrow morning if you'd like."

"Really?" Faith felt hope spread through her. One thing she had missed about back home was going to church on

Sundays and hearing the preacher's message. She missed the singing and she missed the praying and the peace it brought her. "I would love that."

"Your mother and sister are welcome as well," Stephen added, his cheeks growing a bit red, "If they would like to come."

"I will certainly let them know." Faith couldn't stop smiling. "I'll see you tomorrow then."

Faith hurried over to Anna, who she practically had to drag away from the other young girls. They had stayed much too long, but Faith didn't care anymore. She had met Stephan and that had been a great experience in itself. Faith wasn't sure if getting to know him better would be a mistake, but she was willing to find out.

—-*—-

Stephen grinned when he saw Faith and Anna walking up the path. He had gotten used to seeing them every single morning and the little prayer time that he shared with some of the others from the wagon train. The idea of them not showing up made him sad.

He found himself focusing on Faith's radiant smile. The sun was shining off of her light golden hair. Her blue eyes were twinkling, and she looked about as joyful as anything he could imagine.

She and Anna had been coming to meet him for prayer for nearly two weeks now. Every single morning, they would show up a bit early. They would talk for a few minutes, and then they would pray with the other six or seven people who liked to come. After it was done, Stephen would walk them back to their wagon and then spend some time walking beside it with Faith since he was already there. The more he learned about Faith, the more attracted he found himself to her.

"I'm sorry we got up so late. We also have to head back early today," Faith said as soon as they walked up.

"That's perfectly all right. Everyone else just got here." Stephan led the way back to the rest of the group and they got started right away.

Moments when they shared a moment of singing a hymn together or praying together made him feel like he was a little closer to his calling and a little better about leaving his old life behind.

He often thought about his parents and what they must be doing now that he wasn't there anymore.

When the short prayer and song time was over, Stephan motioned for Faith and Anna to follow him.

"Anna was actually planning on staying here for another while to be with her friends," Faith said.

"I'm sure that is fine, and I can help with whatever she would normally do. Why do you need to head back so quickly today?" Stephan felt concerned. He hoped everything was all right with Faith and her family.

"My mother hasn't been feeling so well. I promised I would take over the oxen for a while so she can rest."

"I have most of the day free and know how to drive oxen very well, if you are interested in some help," Stephen offered before he could stop himself. He wasn't sure if he was being too forward with Faith.

She hadn't said anything that made him think she felt the same way about him. He was starting to wonder if he was imagining the connection between them. Or maybe Faith was waiting for him to confess how he was starting to feel to her. But he wasn't exactly sure what sort of feelings he had for her or how to articulate them.

They were certainly more than friendship. But was he ready to have a relationship like that right now? Was he ready to be married with a wife on his new journey in a strange town with so much danger all around them? Those were the things that he was unsure of so he said nothing.

Faith came back from telling Anna that they were heading back to the wagon where her mother was waiting.

"So, how have you liked the new group of wagons compared to the old one?"

"Well, I didn't really have anyone to talk to with the old wagon train." Faith smiled shyly.

"I'm very glad we met then. It has been a pleasure having you and Anna join us in the morning and then of course all of our talks in the afternoons." Stephen scolded himself internally. He was rambling and he was certain that Faith thought he was strange.

It didn't take them long to get back to the wagon. When they did, the two of them climbed up on to the wagon and Faith's mother went to the back to get some rest.

The sound of the oxen's feet against the ground was the only thing that accompanied them as they got situated.

"You never say much about your father. What happened to him?" Stephen asked. He had been wanting to ask her that since the day that they'd met. But he had considered it rude. But now he couldn't keep his curiosity at bay any longer.

"He passed away nearly three years ago in a work accident. He was a logger." Faith sounded sad.

"I'm sorry. You must miss him."

"I do, every day."

Stephen was about to say something else when he caught a glimpse of movement off to the side. Had one of the people from the wagon train wandered off of the road and gone into the woods? It wouldn't be uncommon. They did it often, especially to use the bathroom.

Stephen tried to brush it off and focus his attention on Faith.

But a few seconds later, she was giving him a strange look. "What's wrong? You've been distracted for a while now."

"I... I am not sure. Maybe I was wrong." Stephen shook his head. But just then, he saw the movement again. This time, he saw a flash of a horse deeper in the woods. He was sure of it.

No one from the wagon train would be riding their horse in the woods, would they?

"What is going on? You are starting to scare me." Faith's eyes had gone wide and she did look frightened.

"It is probably nothing, but I think someone is watching the wagons from the woods."

"What?" Faith started to look at the trees.

"Don't look. If it is someone with ill intent, we don't want them to know that we know they are there."

"What are we going to do? What if someone is following us? What are we going to do if they are after us?" Faith was very scared. Stephen felt bad. He hadn't meant to frighten her. But then again, maybe it was necessary. If there was someone after them, they all had to be prepared.

"Faith, you need to go and get your sister. Walk on the inside of the wagons and then bring her directly back here. Have her hide inside the wagon. I am going to go around and let the other men know. Wake your mother and tell her to drive on as if there was nothing to be concerned about. If she has a gun she should keep it with her."

"Okay," Faith nodded and even though she looked pale and terrified, she looked strong and determined.

Stephen reached out and squeezed her hand. "Everything is going to be fine."

Faith gave yet another nod, though she didn't look completely convinced.

Stephen couldn't wait any longer. He knew that if this was a threat like the one that he thought it might be, time was of the essence. He slipped of the wagon on the inside of the trail and walked ahead.

The people in the woods could be bandits, or they could even be Indians. He didn't know, but if they were following the wagon train, that couldn't mean anything good.

Stephen hurried from wagon to wagon. He kept a smile on his face and tried to make it look as if he wasn't doing anything out of the ordinary, He had a couple of men head toward the back of the line of wagons to quietly alert the others.

It took a few moments to convince each of the men. But once they watched the forest for a few minutes, they were quickly convinced that Stephen was right.

The protective side of Stephen wanted to be with Faith. He didn't have any family out here on the wagon train. Faith and her sister felt like the closest thing he had to family.

The worry that he was feeling was mostly for her. He did not know who these people were that were following them. He would guess that they were bandits, but the truth was he didn't know what sort of people they might be up against or when they might attack, and they could pose any sort of threat.

The sun had dipped lower and lower in the sky, and as dusk approached, they decided to stop and make camp. They found a clearing that was up against a canyon wall and made their circle of wagons. They placed their wagons in a tighter circle than usual and put a second row on the outside to make their defense tighter. All of the oxen and horses were in the center and everyone was prepared as they could be to defend themselves.

Tensions were high and they were surrounded by darkness.

"I am going to head back to one of the wagons to make sure Faith and her family are okay," Stephen whispered. He was beside two of the men who were in charge of guiding the wagon train.

They were both ready, beside their wagons with their pistols ready. As far as Stephen knew, he had warned every man in the wagon train. Even though they had gone about preparing for evening as usual, all the men were ready with their weapons and the women cooked together as close to the inside as they could stay.

"You go ahead. Thank you for warning us, Stephen. We would have been blindsided otherwise." Ralf, the guide, gave him a grateful smile.

"I'll see you after it's over, that is if anything happens tonight." Stephen hurried off without waiting for an answer.

Maybe whoever was following them didn't have bad intentions and whoever was out there was simply passing in the woods the same time they were passing on the road.

But Stephen wanted to be by Faith and her family just in case. When he was about halfway back to Faith's wagon, the sound of gunshots in the air made Stephen's hair stand on end.

Torches streamed from the forest. Stephen counted eight of them. Whoever was in the woods did mean them harm, and they were coming.

Stephen forced himself to run faster. His lungs burned and he felt like he would never make it to his destination.

When some of the wagons started to catch fire from the torches, Stephen felt the panic start to set in.

He kept running, but sent up a frantic prayer to God to keep Faith and her family safe.

When he got there, only Faith's mother was outside of the wagon. Their covered wagon had gone up in flames.

"Where's Faith and Anna?" Stephen felt sick. He remembered his last advice to Faith. He had told her to hide in the wagon.

"Anna was in the wagon, Faith went in to help her get out." Faith's mother's eyes were wide with fright.

Anna came squirming out of the flames that had engulfed the wagon. She was coughing and sputtering, looking paler than Stephen had ever seen her before.

"Where's Faith?" Stephen asked.

"She's still in there, something fell on my way out... I-" Anna was taken over by another fit of coughing.

Stephen didn't wait to hear more. He rushed toward the wagon, feeling the heat of the flames as soon as he drew close.

He hurried inside, wincing against the burning sensation on his skin. He wasn't about to let it stop him.

What he saw in the wagon made his heart stop for a second. Faith was there, trapped under a large barrel of flour.

"What are you doing here?" she asked as soon as he was beside her.

"I had to come and make sure you were all right. Don't worry, I am going to get you out of here." He frantically beat at the flames with his coat and tried to fight the panic that threatened to blind him.

—-*—-

Faith had been ready for the possibility of the bandits attacking the wagon train, but she had still ben both terrified and shocked when the men charged at the wagon circle and started setting wagons on fire by throwing their torches.

The men of the wagon train were ready, defending themselves with their pistols and rifles. The men fell from their horses and a cheer went up. But even though they had succeeded in defeating their attackers, several wagons had caught on fire.

Faith swallowed back a cry as she stared up at the covering over the wagon. The flames were quickly consuming the cloth above her. She wondered if she and Stephen would make it out of the burning wagon alive. He was beating at the flames, but they seemed to spread relentlessly down the sides. The torch that had started the fire fell into the wagon with a 'thunk' as it burned through the roof. He grabbed the torch and threw it from the wagon and quickly extinguished the flames that had started the blankets on fire.

"Are you ready? We are going to do this on the count of three." Stephen's voice drew her back to the present.

"I'm ready." Faith bit her lower lip. She was anything but ready, but they had to get the flour barrel off of her leg.

"Okay, one, two, three!" Stephen heaved at the barrel and it lifted just enough for Faith to roll out from under it.

Next thing she knew, Stephen had his hand around her waist and was helping her out and away from the wagon.

Once they were clear, Faith let herself fall to the ground. Stephen continued to beat at the flames on the sides of the wagon until it was just smoking. The covering was gone but it hadn't spread to the wood below.

"Are you okay?" Stephen asked, concern lining his face.

"I think I am. But what are we going to do? Everything we owned was in that wagon."

Stephen shook his head, "I'm sure we can salvage some of it. The top burned off and you lost some bedding but there may be some stuff left. You and your family are welcome to come stay in my wagon. I don't have a lot of things, just a few of the basics. But hopefully enough to keep us all going until we get to town."

"Why would you do that?" Faith asked, her eyes wide. Stephen had been so kind and attentive to her and her family since she'd met him. Her heart beat harder in her chest.

She wanted it to be for a certain reason, but she wasn't sure if she could hope for that or not.

"I would do that because I enjoy your company and also it is the right thing to do... Also, I don't know if this is the right time, but can I ask you something?" Stephen looked as hopeful as Faith felt.

"Of course, what is it?"

"I know we haven't known each other for long. But would you consider getting to know each other a little better? I have never met someone before who I would like to spend my life with, Faith. But I know right now that God put you in my path."

Faith's eyes filled with tears. "I thought you would never ask. And the answer is yes! I would love to get to know you better and then maybe one day, we will marry. We will have to find another preacher to do the honors though."

Stephen chuckled. "You wouldn't mind being a preacher's wife?" he looked a little surprised.

"I would love being a preacher's wife, as long as that preacher was you. I think that it is what God is leading me to do. I never was very keen on marrying a man searching for money with his life. I knew there had to be better priorities than that. And then I met you."

Stephen fell into the grass beside her and the two watched the smoke around them.

Anna and Faith's mother were standing nearby, talking with some concerned people from the other wagons.

Faith heard bits and pieces of their conversation, enough to know that the bandits who had attacked them were either dead or had managed to escape, but that no one had been hurt thanks to the early warning.

"You know, I think that even though my ma doesn't want me to be a preacher, she would like you. Even my pa would. It is nice to know that I am doing something right in their eyes."

Faith smiled. "Do you really think they would like me? When will I meet them?"

"I don't know. Maybe they will come west someday. Or maybe you would like to travel to the city to visit them one day. Preachers travel a lot, you know."

"I know, but I am not sure that I will be ready to take this trip again for a very long time."

"Don't worry, I am sure that we will find other things to occupy our time with for now. Come on, we should get your sister out of the cold night air."

Faith nodded and accepted his hand to stand up.

"Can you walk?" he asked, once again the concern flaring in his eyes.

Eve forced a little nod. "It hurts, but I think it will be fine." She glanced down at the bruised leg that had almost caused her death.

"Okay then. Let's go." Stephen walked ahead with Faith, and Anna and Faith's mother walked behind. Stephen's wagon was rather simple, but he did have a tent and blankets which he gave to Faith and her family, insisting that he would sleep in the wagon.

Before they settled in for the night, Faith leaned against the wagon, staring up at the sky.

"What are you looking at?" Stephen asked, walking up beside her. It reminded her of the first time they had met.

"I was just thinking about how bright the stars are, and how wonderful it is to know that somewhere up there, we are being watched over."

"It is wonderful. I don't know how I would make it through the day without knowing that." Stephen grinned. "And besides watching over me, he has sent me the most beautiful woman in the west."

Faith giggled shyly. "Thank you," she said softly.

The two of them stood there, staring up at the sky, appreciating the beauty of the night. Faith wondered what was waiting for them on the rest of their journey. She knew that whatever it was, they could face it together, with God's guidance.

—-*—-

Faith looked out the window and smiled. She couldn't believe a year had passed so quickly. They had married a few months after arriving in California at a small chapel in the town.

She was happy with how the small cabin had turned out. They had built it together on the edge of a wooded area near a stream and it was a beautiful place to live.

They had built a cabin with two sides, one for them and one for her mother and sister. That way they could each have their own space and farm the ranch together.

She and her mother had started a garden and Stephen had bought two cows and some chickens.

Faith smiled as Stephen came in.

"Are you ready? The wagon is set to go, and we should be back in a few days. The wedding is over in Sunnyvale and we need to be there by tonight to get the chapel ready."

"Yes. Let me say goodbye to Anna and Mama. I'll be right there."

As they started down the trail she looked around at the beauty of the land. Even though there had been trials God had been so good to her giving her far more than she had ever imagined.

She looked at Stephen and smiled. She couldn't imagine life being any better than this.

AMISH AWAKENING

Chapter 1

Hannah stood at the window of her classroom looking out towards the green landscape that stretched out as far as she could see, dark clouds started gathering and was drawing closer with each passing minute. To most those clouds were a sign of new life, but to her it bore nothing but bad memories she simply chose to forget. Father Smith often told her that in order to find peace within herself she would need to make peace with herself, but how could she if it wasn't herself she was angry at? It wasn't her fault that Aaron died.

"Hanna, will you be fine to get home before the storm gets here?" Kemp asked as popping his head in at the class.

Kemp had been a good friend for her, since Aaron's death he had taken it upon himself to be the man of the house, but as Aaron's younger sibling, she felt awkward knowing that he wanted more from her. He may not have said it out loud but his constant fussing over her wellbeing said enough.

"I'll be fine, thank you Kemp, I'm having supper with Father Smith and his family," she said and offered him a friendly smile.

"Of course, well you be careful now," Kemp said and hesitated before turning to leave.

Hannah let out a soft sigh and sent up a silent prayer of thanks. She was growing weary trying to be nice all the time by courteously ignoring Kemp's advances, but some days she itched to just be blatantly rude and tell him to stop trying. But that will cause a few frowns to furrow on the elders' brows. She waited until Kemp was out of sight before she grabbed her basket with her books and left the single structured school building that housed no more than thirty four school children ranging from all ages.

She hurried along the road to get home but the storm was drawing closer faster than expected. Another perfect day ruined, she thought as she treaded ahead, keeping a watchful eye on the clouds rolling in and as the first drops started plummeting down on her she quickened her pace.

The sound of rolling thunder droned in her ears and she clutched her basket tighter, but when an automobile pulled up next to her she realized it was not thunder.

"You won't make it far at this pace *lieb*," the very familiar yet disembodied voice of the driver spoke from inside the car.

"*Lieb*? It is a bad habit making such a personal reference to complete stranger," she said to the man and stepped closer to get a better look at her assailant or her rescuer.

"Greetings Hannah, it's been a long time."

Hannah froze; it was Mason who sat before her as big as life, in an automobile of all things. The last time she had seen him was when she was just seventeen. He had always been the black sheep in the community, disobeying so many of the rules, that by the time he turned eighteen he decided to venture into the great big modern world, and disappeared from her life.

"Mason Smith," she said and smiled, "you have not changed one bit."

He threw his head back and laughed, "In this light you cannot see my grey hairs. Now are you going to walk the rest of the way home, or will you let me take you."

She swayed and looked down at her feet, contemplating a ride. She was sure that it will just loosen a few tongues if she arrived home with him.

"*Denki*, but I think I will walk, it's not too far now," she declined and stepped away from the automobile, "I'm sure to see you at your father's house?"

Mason smiled and nodded at her, "That depends if my father will welcome me into his house."

"The Prodigal son returns," she said raising her shoulders and tucking them forward as the rain started to pelt down around her, "I'll see you later."

Instead of running along the road, she chose to run across the fields towards her house and away from Mason. Seeing him after all these years should not have caused such a kaleidoscope of butterflies to wreak havoc in her stomach but it has. She had noticed the slight grey hair peppered against his temples and the increased amount of laughing lines that deepened next to his eyes when he smiled. He had also no beard, which meant that he had not yet been wed, but then again, the modern worlds' cultures are far different to their own simple way of life, and the mere thought left her wondering where he had been all these years.

By the time she reached her house, she was completely drenched right through to her undergarments. She suddenly felt nervous to attend supper with the Smiths' but unless she was ill she could not come up with an honest enough excuse as to why she can't attend. She was going to have to just try and act as normal as possible around Mason, that is if his father allows him to sit with them.

Chapter 2

Mason left the community just after his eighteenth birthday, and the day he left, his father told him that he would wait for him. Personally he never thought he would come back here, but life has the tendency to throw curveballs when least expected. And from personal experience the curve balls just keep coming.

He hardly expected to see Hannah, or rather he expected that she would still be here, but he didn't expect their run in with each other to have such an effect on him. Even when he approached her from a distance, his gut told him that it was Hannah walking alongside the road. Call it providence or pure chance, but he would recognize her from every angle simply by the way she walked. She had this distinct way of walking on her toes while hardly moving her arms. Now years after experiencing the modern world, her walk reminded him a ballerina, precise and delicately calculated and all his memories came flooding back.

When she ran across the field he couldn't help but smile, knowing that she too had a moment of dejavu and for a moment he silently wished he never left, but he knew if he did stay it would have been for her only and he simply could not tie himself down to a life of common needs and simplicity, he was too eager to explore the world.

As he pulled up to his fathers' house he looked up at the house, as usual well kept, but a simple uncomplicated structure, like their way of life here in Lancaster. He remembered his life here as if it was yesterday, and although he had an enquiring and curious mind, he had to admit that staying here would have prevented many complications in his life. His cell phone vibrated on his dash but he chose to ignore it, instead he shoved it in the glove compartment and got out of the car.

"Mason!" his mother cried out as she came running down the stairs hugging him tight.

His father stood at the stop of the stairs with his arms crossed and a deadpan expression that would put a corpse to shame, but then again his father was never one to show any emotion unless it was to hand out corporal punishment and of that he had more than his fair share.

"*Mamm*, it's good to see you," he said and hugged his mother. She had gotten old and although she appeared relaxed he could see that life and labour had taken its toll.

"Mason my son, please come inside, we are so happy to have you here," his mother said excitedly.

"*Daed*, how are you?" he asked his father boldly.

"We're fine, ya," his father responded flatly and stood aside for him to enter.

Nothing had changed since he initially left for his Rumspringa, which he never returned from, and being back after so many years, was like a time traveling experience.

"Lydia is married now," his mom said as she set a space for him at the dinner table.

"I know, she wrote me."

His mother and father exchanged looks and then went on as if he never said a word.

"She's with child, and the baby should be here within the month or so."

Clearly his father did not approve of his sister writing to him, so instead he smiled, "I will make an effort to congratulate her when I see her."

The awkward silence was followed with a light knock and when he turned around to see who it was, he was pleasantly surprized to find Hannah standing in the doorway.

"Mason, Hannah has dinner with us every Friday evening," his mother said and gestured for Hannah to sit down.

Mason turned to her, "Do you not have a family of your own?"

"Let's say grace," Mason's father interrupted and he immediately could have kicked himself for asking such a personal question. Now that he was back among his family he had to be careful of what he said and how he said things.

They all took hands and while his father said grace, Mason was acutely aware of Hannah's hand in his. He could feel her fingers trembling in his and he smiled. He made her nervous; he could only hope it was the good kind of nervous.

After dinner they all sat at the table while Hannah and Mrs Smith gathered the dishes and took it to the kitchen.

"How long are you planning on visiting?" Mason's father asked.

"Not sure, at the moment it's indefinitely."

A loud crash sounded from the kitchen, and his father's intense gaze held his.

"Indefinitely is a long time."

"Depending on the inevitability of it," Mason said.

"You're room is still as it was, your mother never changed it. She waited for you."

"At least someone did."

He held his father's gaze and then stood up and excused himself. He had to give his father time; he had been away for such a long time, with little or no contact. But then again if they were just a little bit more open minded towards the use of modern technology he would have been in constant contact with his family. The few letters he exchanged with his sister was hard enough to keep up with, as it stands, people no longer wrote letters and wasted their time with postage, they e-mailed or chatted to each other.

"I'll get my things from the car," Mason said and excused himself from the table.

Chapter 3

Hannah spent the entire evening seated next to Mason trying her best not to breathe, or inhale the intoxicating smell that filled her nostrils every time he moved. The odd time she visited town she often took a sneaky sniff of the perfumes that were sold, more to remind her just how much power there was in such an evil cheap substance, or so she told herself. But now here next to Mason, the smell turned from offensive to hallucinogenic. Every time she found herself leaning towards him and then she had to recite a bible verse that reminded her of infidelity and the sinful nature of the flesh. I shall not want, she kept saying to herself mentally and when Mrs Smith got up and started to clear the table, she was only too thankful to join her and get away from the magnetic pull that was threatening to ruin her.

That was until she heard Mason mention that his stay was indefinite. That meant she was going to see him every single day until he decides to run away again.

The words came as such a shock that she dropped the plate she was holding. Mrs Smith was quick to bend down and help her pick up the broken pieces.

"He has changed," she said to Hannah, "but he's still my son."

"The world tends to change a person," Hannah whispered and smiled at the older woman with the sad blue eyes.

She remembered the day they realized Mason was not going to come back, his mother was in tears for days, while his father put up this façade of callous indifference. But she knew they missed their son.

"Hannah, you can make him see the truth."

That was a tall order; Hannah thought and tossed the glass into the bin.

"I don't think it is my place to convince him," she said.

"You're right I'm sorry, I just – I don't want him to leave again."

Hannah could understand how Mason's mother must have felt, for someone to leave for such a long time is almost like sending someone off to the beyond. But how was she going to convince him to stay, he had experienced the modern world and drove an automobile not to mention that he used men's perfume. Why would he trade that freedom for this?

"I think I need to head home Mrs Smith, I still have a quilt to finish before Sunday," she said and gathered her coat, "I'll be seeing you."

"Of course dear, but do come around when you want some company."

"I sure will."

Hannah was tucked under her blanket in front of the fireplace and had just started to quilt when there was a slight knock on the door. What a strange time for a visitor, she thought as she went to open the door.

"Mason," she said shocked.

"Hannah, may I come in?"

"I-I don't think it's proper for me to invite you in," she said and reached for her shawl, and then stepped outside, closing the door behind her.

"I understand, I just thought you could use some company," he said with a smile that tugged at the corners of his mouth.

She felt her stomach tumble again and she took a deep steadying breath.

"We can go for a walk," she offered.

"Sure." Mason held out his arm but instead she wrapped her arms around herself.

"Why did you come back?"

"It's a long story."

One he would most likely not want to share with her, but she was curious as to why he was back. What if he was running from the law, she thought slightly panicked, but she couldn't see him to be someone who would use this community as a curtain to hide behind.

"We'll time is what I have. You left here in such a hurry, and now after I don't know even how long, you're back like a ghost from the past."

"Maybe I am a ghost, and I decided to come and haunt you," he said and laughed.

Hannah also laughed and shook her head, "A lot has changed since you left."

"Like what, a few more babies born and a few sad souls sent to the hereafter? Come on Hannah, nothing changes amongst the Amish, you know that."

"Well I got married," she said and when he stopped she turned to look at him.

"And you're here walking with me, what will your husband have to say?"

"He's no longer here; he passed away," *and I'm grateful he did*, she thought not voicing her true feelings. What would Mason have said if he knew Aaron's true colours?

"So who was he?"

"Who was who?"

"Your husband, who was the lucky guy?"

"Aaron."

An awkward silence settled between them and Hannah bit her lip. Even when they were teenagers, Mason and Aaron always competed to gain her attention. They were the trio of friends who did everything together as kids, and as they got older she always thought she would marry Mason the day they were old enough. But the day Mason left he broke her heart, she waited for him to return but he never did and eventually she gave in and married Aaron, thinking they would have a happy life. But Aaron wasn't the same fun loving boy she knew or maybe he knew all along that he was just a plaster for her broken heart, a replacement for Mason, which is why he was so angry with her all the time.

"Was he good to you?" Mason asked as if he could read her mind.

"He was a good man," she responded averting her eyes.

"That was not my question Hannah," he said and took her by the shoulders, "was he good to you?"

In the moonlight she could see the flecks of silver in his blue eyes, and her heart ached with longing. But this was not right, no matter what her heart and body wanted, in her mind she was determined that she would not lust after another man. Yes she was a widow and yes, she may remarry, but that thought had never crossed her mind. Only now with Mason back she had dabbled with the idea of having her happily ever after, but it was only a dream. Just like the dream she had when she was only sixteen. And from experience all dreams eventually fade and turn into a cruel reality.

She pulled away from him and turned around to head back to the house.

"I do not wish to discuss Aaron with you," she blurted out as she felt tears sting her eyes, "Go home Mason, your mother will be worried about you."

Chapter 4

Mason had this strange feeling that Aaron had turned out to be exactly what he always thought. As young men they both loved Hannah, and although they never showed it in the open there was a sort of rivalry between them. The day he decided to go on a Rumspringa, Aaron had thanked him for leaving, and Mason had felt as if he had betrayed Hannah, but Aaron was also his friend and at the time he figured he'll be the lesser one and allow his friend a fair chance, hoping that Hannah will calm the anger in Aaron. Aaron was your average young man, but he had an angry and cruel disposition, when no-one was watching he was the one who threw stones at new born lambs and shot birds out of the trees with a sling shot, simply for the fun of it. Even his mother had to deal with his insubordination, but in front of the rest of the community he was the son everyone wished for.

Mason felt a cold stab of regret at the thought of Aaron hurting Hannah and knowing that he was indirectly to blame, made him feel sick. He had to find out what she had gone through and try and fix what he had broken, but with the hands of time waiting for no one, he wouldn't even know where to start, or whether it was too late for a new beginning.

He set off after Hannah as she rushed back to the house.

"Hannah wait!" he called but she didn't turn, she just walked straight ahead.

"Hannah!"

"Go home Mason," she said sternly but as she reached for the door handle he placed his hand over hers.

"Did he hurt you?"

He felt her back straighten and her entire body go rigid, her actions confirming his suspicions.

"Oh my god, I'm so sorry," he said and squeezed her shoulder with his other hand.

She turned in his arms and her eyes were cold and hard as she looked at him.

"Do not use the Lords name in vain."

Right, he was among very religious people now, he had to count his words and check his actions all the time.

"I'm sorry, it's a bad habit, but I am truly sorry," he said and then pulled her in to hug her.

"Mason, please," he heard her plead against his chest, "why don't you go back to where you came from?"

Was she so mad at him that she wanted him to leave? He knew he probably didn't deserve her time but surely she could understand that they were all young and he was curious about the world. She could have gone with him when he asked her but she was too scared to set foot outside of this protected cocoon of a life she was too familiar with.

"That's not happening in a hurry sweetheart," he said and tilted her chin up, "I'm here to stay, for a while."

When she looked up at him he was tempted to kiss her, but instead he took a step back.

"I'll be seeing you at Church on Sunday," he said and then tipped his hat and made his way home.

He had to keep reminding himself that life amongst the Amish wasn't anything like the world out there; he had to watch his tongue and try his best not to be tempted by a beautiful woman. As it were, temptation had caused him enough headaches to last him a life time.

He looked at his phone and grimaced. Roxanne had been phoning him non-stop, and he had no desire to return her calls and if he had a penny left he would pay her to go away. She deceived him, made him believe she was in love with him, and then tricked him into making him believe she was with child. He had found out by chance that she was lying to him, and when he did it was the last straw. It was that, which finally made him realize that the world he had chosen to embrace was nothing but a place where people are self-centred and illogical. None of his worldly friends or rather foes knew where he was, he had also turned off his location based service on his phone in case anyone wanted to track him down.

If he was going to make a change and revert back to the old ways of the Amish, he was going to have to consider getting rid of his electronic devices, but he wasn't so sure if he was willing to part with his music. That was the one thing he had grown to enjoy about life on the outside, while here amongst the Amish musical instruments were forbidden.

Chapter 5

A week has passed since Mason's arrival in Lancaster, and Hannah had done everything in her power to avoid him. Not because she disliked him or because she was angry with him, but because he stirred emotions she had completely forgotten about. She spent hours on her knees praying that the Lord take away the feelings that she harboured.

She glanced at herself in the mirror once again and sighed. Why does she even bother about her appearance, it was not like her to be so vain, but she's spent more time in front of the mirror in the past week than she did in her entire life. She rolled her plated hair into a bun and pinned it to her head before putting on her bonnet, she had to get over this stupid notion that there could be anything between her and Mason. He was a confused man with a foot in both worlds, and if he was not able to decide where he belonged how was she going to fit into his world anyway. Tonight she was going to be attending the sing, and she knew for a fact that Mason would be there too. Her stomach tumbled again and she clutched the front of her dress and sighed heavily. The sooner she got this over with the better, but as she exited the house, he was waiting for her. He had borrowed his father's buggy and was even wearing traditional Amish clothes.

"I was about to come and find you," he said and smiled.

"You wouldn't have had to look far."

"Indeed, you look beautiful."

Hannah felt her cheeks flame up and she quickly looked down and cleared her throat. Why after all these years did he still have this effect on her?

"Thank you."

"Can I offer you a ride to the Sing?"

"I was- I was going to take a walk, I enjoy the fresh air," she lied and shifted her weight.

"Are you going to avoid me for the rest of your life?"

"I don't know what you mean."

"You avoided me at church service; you hide in your class room every day. I'm not a bad man Hannah," he said and came to stand before her.

"I'm not avoiding you, I'm a busy woman," *and dead scared that the feelings I have will be unrequited,* she thought.

"Lying is as great a sin as blasphemy, so why don't you tell me why you are avoiding me?"

Hannah rolled her eyes and stepped past him, "We're going to be late, and I don't have time for idle chit chat."

"We're not going anywhere until you tell me what you are afraid of," he insisted and caught her arm.

She felt a shiver run down her spine as his hand wrapped around her upper arm, and although her sleeve offered some resistance it still felt as if his fingers were touching her bare skin.

Should she tell him what really scared her, and admit to him that she still had feelings for him despite the fact that she had given herself to Aaron all those years ago? Should she tell him how Aaron took his anger outbursts out on her and caused her to lose their child? The day she was promised to Aaron her nightmare started, although she could not deny him physically she hated every intimate moment with him. He took what he wanted when he wanted, and if she wasn't responsive enough he would get physically abusive with her. It took her a good few years to finally get over her fears and make peace with what had happened. The community never spoke a word about it although they all knew, and even when the elders got involved nothing was done.

"Get in the buggy, I'll take you to the sing," he said and led her to the carriage.

"It's not appropriate," she said and tugged her arm free.

"We're adults, not teenagers," he said and then softened his tone, "It's just a ride to my father's house."

She sighed and then got into the buggy, with her hands folded tightly on her lap.

The drive to the sing was cloaked in complete silence, and it felt as if she was suffocating with words that were trying to force their way up in her throat. She had to just get through this evening and keep calm, she kept telling herself, but she knew that it was not going to be that easy. Mason kept looking at her and she could feel his gaze rest on her face.

"Staring at me is not going to change anything," she said and looked directly at him. If he wasn't going to get the hint she was going to have to be honest with him.

He pulled the carriage to a halt and turned to her and unexpectedly cupped her face and pressed his lips against hers. For a moment she froze as his lips pressed against hers, then suddenly that intoxicated musky scent filled her senses. Her defences weakened instantly and she willingly parted her lips, but as his tongue touched hers she pulled away and jumped out of the buggy and ran.

"Lord, forgive me, I have sinned," she prayed and rushed across the field towards the Smiths' house. How could she have been so weak to allow a man to seduce her? But even as guilt flooded her, she kept thinking of his kiss and memories of a long time ago flooded her mind.

The day before he left he had kissed her, not like he kissed her tonight, but it was a kiss that remained with her all these years. A kiss she tucked away in the confines of her mind, and now that, that memory had resurfaced she felt confused and uncertain.

By the time she got to the Sing, Mason's carriage was already there. She composed herself as much as she could before entering the house. He was nowhere to be seen, but the house was full of young eager teenagers, happily singing their songs of worship. Although the event had nothing to do with devotion it was one of the more sociable events, where all the young people normally got to socialize.

She made her way through to the kitchen and joined the older women where they were preparing food.

"Did Mason fetch you?" Mrs Smith asked as she came to stand next to Hannah.

"He did come around, but I walked here instead," she said softly.

"He fancies you Hannah," she said as she moved closer, almost whispering.

"I know, I just don't know if it's appropriate. He hasn't been among us for so long and people will talk."

"You're a widow, Aaron is gone and I can guarantee you that no one will be raising any brows at you."

Hannah sighed, if it wasn't Mason it was his mother, but she knew that someone in the community would have something to say about such a union.

During the sing, Hannah was intensely aware of Mason's presence, but what made it worst was that Kemp was also there, and it suddenly felt like a bad case of dejavu with a very familiar love triangle forming, but Kemp was not aware of Mason's intent. Sooner or later he was going to realize it and then she would be stuck in the middle.

Before the sing was over, she snuck out, hoping that she left undetected, but her luck had run out.

"Hannah," it was Kemp who fell into step beside her, "You're leaving so early, are you not feeling well?"

"Oh no, I'm fine, I'm just a little tired."

She was lying again, she was going to go straight to hell at this rate, she thought to herself.

"Let me get the carriage and I'll take you home."

"No!" she all but shouted, and then toned her voice down, "I mean, no thank you. I'd rather walk."

The look on Kemp's face was one of concern but he didn't push, he simply smiled, "I'll keep you company then."

She was growing weary with this whole avoiding men thing, at this point she felt as if she was a lamb being cornered by a pack of wolves and she hated every minute of it. On the one hand Kemp was a nice man, the complete opposite of Aaron, but he was just too familiar to her. And then there was Mason, who she had feelings for since the age of fourteen. This was all too much.

"Hannah, we've known each other for a long time, and I was thinking we should consider a future together," he said out of the blue.

"Uh-I, I'm not sure I understand?"

"I want to marry you," Kemp said without blinking.

If she had a mouth full of food, she would have choked right this minute. This was a little sudden, and she knew why he had moved so quickly, he must feel threatened with Mason back in town.

"Kemp, you're a wonderful man, but I don't see a future with you, we've had too much history and having been married to Aaron makes it awkward."

"How so?" he asked as he took her hand in his.

She pulled her hand away, "It just does, if I was to marry again, it would be for love and what we have is just a friendship, which I value."

The disappointment on his face saddened her, but she could not lie and pretend that she saw a future with him. She stood and watched as he finally walked away from her before she continued to her house, but as she reached her door, Mason appeared out of the shadows.

"So it's Kemp?" he asked blankly.

"Excuse me?"

"Kemp, you wouldn't even allow me to take you to the sing because you don't want him to see you with me."

"First of all, it is not Kemp, we are just friends and secondly the reason I walked to the sing was because you kissed me. You had no right," she said angrily.

"You enjoyed that kiss as much as I did, why do you deny it?"

Hannah unlocked her door and then turned to Mason, "This is not a forsaken place like the city Mason, we have values, I have values and if you cannot respect that then there is no place for you here."

Mason approached her and stopped so close she could inhale his very breath.

"Do you have feelings for me, because if you don't, I need to know and stop wasting my time."

"Why? It's not as if you're planning on staying here, you'll leave just like you did all those years ago and I'm sorry Mason, but I will not subject myself to such disappointment again."

She didn't wait for his response simply entered the house and shut the door behind her. Regardless of the condition of her heart, she was not going to leave it out in the open to be trampled on again. The ball was in his court now, if he really was interested in her. He would have to prove himself.

Chapter 6

Mason spent a week contemplating his future, and every time he saw Hannah, he was more and more convinced that he would not leave a second time, and after consulting with his father and the other elders, they agreed to baptize him into the church. He may have been gone longer than most, but he was never officially shunned from the community. And regardless of his life style in the city, they opted to overlook his error in judgement.

It was a private affair with only the elders and his close family around to witness the baptism, and once it was over, he decided to go to the school and wait for Hannah. When she exited the school his heart skipped a beat, it was quite strange how his own emotions were suddenly so intensified after the baptism, he had often wondered if this baptism really changed anyone, but now he knew beyond the shadow of a doubt he was a new person. He had died down his old life and was willing to walk the straight and narrow with Hannah by his side if she let him.

"Afternoon Hannah," he said as she reached him.

"Mason, what brings you here?"

He smiled and took his hat off, "I wanted to come see you."

She smiled and tucked a lose strand of hair behind her ear, "Is that so?"

Even Hannah looked different now, it was as if this cloud of fog that kept skewed his outlook on life had been lifted, "Yes indeed, would you like to go for a walk with me?"

He saw her hesitate slightly but then she nodded, "Of course, I could use some fresh air before I have to go to the sisters meeting."

They walked in silence for a short while and as if they were both searching for words they spoke at the exact same time, "I wanted...." Mason started.

"What did you..." Hannah interrupted and then giggled.

"Well, it spent some time thinking about what you said."

Bending down he picked a small yellow flower and then handed it to her, "I have decided to stay here in Lancaster. My father was willing to baptize me so I'm once again part of the community."

The look on her face was priceless, and the way her eyes lit up made him want to kiss her there and then, but he refused to ruin a perfect moment.

"You did?" she asked breathlessly.

"Yes, you see, I left here thinking that the world was what I needed, and for some time it was fun, but after I returned here and saw you again, I realized what a big mistake that was."

He could tell she didn't know what to say by the way her mouth fell opened and closed, so he continued, "Hannah, I know a lot has happened and you're afraid of commitment, but I've always loved you and I want to spend the rest of my life proving that to you."

"Mason..." she started and looked down at the flower in her hand, "what if you decide to leave again?"

"I won't, my life is here now, my family and friends, and I want to be where you are." He stepped closer and cupped the side of her face, "Only if that is what you want."

Hannah leaned into his touch and a single tear ran down the side of her cheek which he wiped with the pad of his thumb.

"Do you promise to stay?" she asked in a trembling voice.

"I promise."

"Good because my heart would never survive if you broke it a second time," she said and walked into his arms.

"I'll protect it with my life."

****

Four months later, Hannah and Mason finally got married. Mason had laid down his former life and found his own feet amongst his fellow Amish folk, but he would never have been able to do this without Hannah. She was his beacon in his dark night.

lone moon ranch

PART ONE

She felt a mix of relief and despair as she watched the Boston skyline fade away. She felt a mix of relief and despair. She knew she would never come back to her beloved hometown. There was nothing left for her there. In fact, all she had left fit into a small carry-on bag. Her life had shattered, and most of the pieces had blown away in the wind.

She grabbed her phone and read Colt's email again.

I am a simple man. I own the Lone Moon Ranch in Helena, Montana. I've lived here all my life. I am 26 now. I am looking for a wife, someone who can take over the household duties; cooking, cleaning and such. Also, to assist with various chores around the ranch. I need someone who is not deterred by early mornings and not afraid of hard work. In return, I will make sure you are well-taken care of. I am seeking a partner, not a companion. Please contact me if you have questions.

He didn't include a photo and she never asked for one. It didn't matter what he looked like. She appreciated the fact that he sounded very businesslike in his email. That's what this was – a business deal. She had placed an ad on a mail order bride site - not for love, but for security. Colt fit the bill. He needed a wife and she needed an escape. Of course, he had no clue what she was escaping from. She hadn't been completely honest with him about her past.

She tossed her phone back into her purse. She rubbed her thumb against her ring finger as she laid back against her seat and closed her eyes. She didn't want to think about Nick. But he was always there, lurking just below the surface. She could picture his dark eyes and dangerous smile. When they met, he made her feel alive and invincible. Loving Nick was like grabbing hold of a lightning bolt. He had lit her up and then burned her to ashes.

They got married a month after their first date. Nick was wild and impulsive that way, and she couldn't deny him anything. But Nick was also a drunk and a gambler. He got so wasted on their wedding night that he passed out in the hotel lobby. Three months in, he had blown through all her savings. He became violent and erratic when the money ran out. He isolated her from her family and her friends so she had no one to help her. And she couldn't leave him. They were each other's obsession even though he scared her. But then one night he crashed into another car and almost killed the driver. She could picture his face the day of sentencing. Six years. And the way he looked at her the last time she went to visit him, to tell him she had filed for divorce. She lied to him and told him it was all his fault. But she couldn't lie to herself. She knew she was just as much to blame. Maybe he struck the match but they had both danced within the flames.

Their 2-year marriage had stripped her of everything. She lost her condo, her car, and even her job. Her parents had both passed way, and both her brother and sister had given up on her. She needed to start over. And there were worst ways to do that than a beautiful ranch in Montana. So, she bought a plane ticket and a new dress using the only credit card she had left and swore to do her very best to not look back.

***

Colt Malone stood inside Helena Regional Airport. He jiggled his truck keys impatiently against his thigh. Joelle's flight had been delayed. And while he was many things, patient was not one of them. It was a trait that had never come easily to him. Mainly because he rarely liked to be idle.

Nearly every woman that walked past him, smiled. Women had always noticed him. But it had been a long time since one had shared his life or his bed. Not since Ashlyn. They had grown up together. He chased her from the moment he was big enough to run. He couldn't recall a moment of his life that he didn't love her. She had been his best friend and then his lover. But Ashlyn wanted to chase something of her own. Her dreams had taken her far from Montana and far from him. She was in California now. He used to think they'd get married and build a life together. He used to think love matter more than anything. Now he knew better. Love broke you in ways that would never heal. And he didn't intend to ever give someone that kind of power over him again.

He made the ranch his whole life. His father had died three years prior, and he had no other family. When his father died, the ranch and all the responsibility of it became his. It was a huge undertaking. The ranch was financially in bad shape. It was burden his father had never shared with him, but something he inherited just the same.

Things still weren't great. He worked from sun up to sun down, but the ranch was still in jeopardy. He had to lay off most of the staff. He had taken out new loans to pay off old ones. But the ranch was still in debt. He knew he didn't have time to be angry but he was. He was angry that his father hadn't been a better businessman. He was angry at his mother for leaving when he was young. He was angry at the hand life and love had dealt him.

He couldn't say what came over him the night he went online and found the mail order bride website. He guessed it was his loneliness. He wanted to come home to a hot meal and a warm body. He didn't want someone to fall in love with but he did want a partner. Someone to share his burdens and his life. Joelle's ad had stood out to him. She was beautiful but haunted. Long, dark hair and big expressive eyes. She looked like a painting from another time and place. She seemed like a woman that could possess a man and make him beg at her feet, and yet gave him the sense that she didn't want to possess anyone. What she wanted was security. A place in the world that belonged to her. He could give her that, even if he could never give her his heart.

The gate opened, and a rush of people came toward him. Cole scanned the crowd looking for her. He had looked at her picture a dozen times. He had stared into her hazel eyes and memorized the color of her lips and the curve of her neck. His finger had traced each wave of her long, raven hair. But that picture had in no way prepared him for the real-life version.

He called her name and she walked toward him, her cheeks flush and her hair slightly tangled. She was smiling, but it didn't quite reach her eyes.

"Colt?"

"Hello," he said. His voice came out slightly gruff.

"Hi." She hesitated for a moment, but then sat down her bag and leaned into him.

He didn't think, he just put his arms around her and closed his eyes. He felt his whole body respond to hers, full and warm against him. She smelled of a lavender and citrus. And when she pulled back to look up at him, he felt breathless for the first time in a long time. Yep, she could awaken a hunger in a man and he was in no way immune; and it was a hunger he had almost forgotten was there. His pulse quickened, and this animal desire to ravage her was stirring inside. He swallowed, and took a long, shaky breath.

"I'm glad I'm here," she said softly.

"So am I."

They stood for a moment, still half in each other's arm. He took another breath and steadied himself.

"We should get going Do you have more bags?" he asked.

She smiled again in a sad sort of way. He saw something in her eyes for the briefest of moments, but then it was gone.

"This is all I have." She gestured toward the bag at her feet. "I meant it when I said I was looking forward to a fresh start."

He picked up the bag for her. "My trucks just outside then," he said. "We have an appointment at the courthouse in less than an hour."

She nodded. They had done the paperwork online, and obtain their marriage license. He had told her he didn't see any reason to put things off, and so he made an appointment at the courthouse for them to be married that afternoon. She didn't seem to want to wait either.

They exited the airport and Joelle's breath hitched as she took in the landscape. The blue sky was cloudless and seemed to have no end. The land before them was flat and rugged until your eyes found the mountains jutting into the heavens.

"It's so beautiful," she said softly.

"It is," he agreed. He had never strayed far from home. The soul of him came from the land and those mountains.

They reached his pickup truck, and he tossed her bag into the bed of it. The truck was painted a fire engine red and it was well loved and taken care of.

"After you." He opened the passenger side door, and then without thinking he reached down and touched her cheek. This made her lips part slightly.

An invitation?

Her lips were as red as his truck and he couldn't seem to look away. Slowly he bent down, letting his own lips graze her's. His hands fell to her waist, and he pulled her body to his. He kissed her, tasting the sweetness of her. She didn't respond to him at first. But he felt the exact moment when she let go. She molded herself to him, and her body hummed. She made a sexy, breathy sound and it about did him in. Somehow he knew she had the same kind of demons that he did. She buried things too. Maybe like him, she still held out hope that one day she'd find redemption.

She pulled away first. She stared at him, her breath ragged.

"Colt, I didn't come here to fall for you."

Trying to regain his composure he said, "I didn't bring you here to fall in love."

"Before we do this, I need you to promise me again. Love is not part of the agreement."

"I do. And I'll keep my promise." He nodded toward the open truck door and ran his fingers through his hair. She was holding his gaze, searching.

"So will I," she said and got up into the truck. They were on the road a moment later, heading for the courthouse on the other side of town.

***

Joelle tried to stop her hands from shaking. She and Colt had arrived at the courthouse, and she could hear the Judge and Colt talking. But all she could think of was that moment she spotted him in the airport. He had on a pair of Wrangler's that fit him well and a button-down shirt. Cowboy boots of course and she had spotted a matching cowboy hat in the truck. He was also sporting a five o'clock shadow even though it was only noon. He wore it well. Too well. He was quite possibly the most handsome man she had even laid eyes on. His auburn hair that curled at the ends and those smoky eyes rimmed with lashes that went on for days. And when he kissed her...

"We're ready." Colt touched her arm lightly. The Judge was just beside him.

"But are you ready my dear?" he asked. He had a soft voice and a kindly face.

"I do – I mean I am," she stammered. They both smiled at her and she laughed nervously. Colt had her undone and that was not part of the plan.

The simple ceremony took less than ten minutes. When it concluded, Colt leaned in and kissed her again. This kiss was softer and sweeter. It held a promise instead of passion. It told her he would be there and he would take care of her.

"Let's go home," he said.

It was a good twenty minutes before they reached the ranch. Colt turned down a rocky drive. Lone Moon Ranch sat a mile off the main road with rolling hills on either side. The main house was average in size, painted red with a white a trim. A barn sat directly to the left of the house, and acres of pasture and field to the right. She breathed in the smell of cut grass and watched as hundreds of dandelions danced in the late afternoon breeze. She spotted several cows in the pasture, and could make out the sound of horses nearby.

He put the car in park right in front of the house. He got out and came around to open the door for her. They stood in the driveway for a long time in silence. He was letting her take everything in. She had never seen so much land and beauty in all her life. She felt like she had been dropped in the middle of nowhere, and the middle of nowhere looked a lot like paradise.

"Hello!" A middle-aged woman came down the front porch steps. She was drying her hands on the apron she wore. Her graying hair was pulled back into a tight bun, and she had a big smile on her face. She came toward Joelle, and pulled her into a tight hug.

"My goodness, you are gorgeous." She pulled back, holding Joelle at arm's length. Then she leaned in and hugged her again. "We are so happy to have you. And congratulations to you both!" She turned to him then, and he bent so she could kiss his cheek. She looked at him with such affection that it made Joelle smile.

"This is Minnie," Colt said. "Minnie, this is Joelle."

"You can call me Jo."

Minnie turned back and hugged her again.

"Minnie is a dear friend," he explained. "She comes by once or twice a week to help tidy up or cook one of her delicious meals. I don't deserve her at all, but I honestly don't know what I would do without her."

"Oh shush." She slapped him playfully on the arm. "I love you like my own son. And how I wish I could do more for you, love." Her eyes got misty. "But here you are now." She turned back to Joelle. "I am just so happy that Colt has found someone to love again."

Colt cleared his throat uncomfortably and she got the impression that Minnie had no idea how they had met. And maybe she would be a bit taken aback if she knew he had basically gone online and ordered up a bride.

"Well, I am happy to be here. So happy," Joelle said. "Colt has just stolen my heart and I don't ever want it back."

Minnie clapped her hands in delight, smiling brightly at them. He was giving her a look, and she gave him a sideways smile.

"Well, come on in. You must be tired and famished. I have dinner all ready." She directed them inside, like a shepherd herding her flock.

Once inside the house, she took a moment to look around her new home. All the rooms were big and open, with high ceilings and lots of windows. The living room was to her left, and a large stone fireplace stood against the back wall. He didn't have a whole lot of furniture, a leather couch, and two big chairs.

She made her way to the kitchen, which was also airy and full of lots of natural light. A large island sat in the center and a small breakfast nook in the corner. The dining room sat off to the right, and both rooms blended well together.

"There's a roast warming in the oven. And biscuits on the table," Minnie said. "You've outdone yourself again," he told her.

"Oh, don't fuss on me. You sit down and enjoy your dinner. I'll be around tomorrow, Jo, to help you settle in."

"Thank you – so much," she said.

Minnie smiled and touched her cheek. "You're going to be very happy here," she promised and then she was gone.

He glanced toward the dining room table. "Shall we?" he asked.

She nodded, her stomach rumbling at the thought. She hadn't eaten breakfast or lunch that day. In fact, she hadn't eaten much at all lately. Certainly, nothing that resembled a home cooked meal.

They ate in silence for several minutes. She savored the biscuits dipped in honey. She glanced up at him, the late afternoon sun poured in through a window, and she could see the flecks of red in his hair.

"I'm sorry you didn't have any family or friends here today," he said.

"I don't have a family. None that speak to me anyway. And no real friends either," she told him. "It's just me."

"Why doesn't your family speak to you?" he asked.

She looked up, meeting his gaze. "My parents died last year. It was a car accident. That sent my spiraling a bit. I didn't always make the best decisions. My brother and sister are both older than me. I guess they handle things better than I do. She has two kids and he owns his own business. I'm the black sheep and they finally threw in the towel."

"Doesn't seem fair," he said. "You're family. They shouldn't just turn their backs on you."

"I don't blame them," she replied honestly. "I hurt them a lot. They felt like they needed to protect themselves."

He sat back in his chair, holding her gaze across the table. "Is that why you left? Why you married me?"

"I don't have anything, Colt. I'm embarrassed to say that, but it's the truth. But now I'm your wife. And here we are together, and I want this to work. I want this ranch to be as much mine as it is yours. I want us to take care of it together."

"And you mean that?"

"I do."

"You know, it's just me, too. Sure – I have friends. Wonderful friends. But no family. This ranch is all I have, and I work every day to hold on to it for me... For us." He paused still watching her. "And I'm sorry about your parents. I never knew my mother, but my daddy passed away three years ago. So, I mean it – I am sorry."

"It's been over a year. You would think it would hurt a little less by now."

"It won't ever hurt any less. You just learn to live with it."

They took their time finishing dinner. She liked talking to him and he seemed to like to listen. She talked a lot about Boston. It was her first love after all. They also talked about the ranch, and she asked him questions about his life growing up.

When they finished, he stood and pushed his chair back heavily. "I get up at five. We should go to bed."

Bed?

His eyes had turned to smolder. Slowly, she stood as well.

"Okay."

"Jo, listen - I've never had a woman in my bed who didn't want to be there," he began. "But it's been a long time. So, I am hoping you will join me in it tonight." With that, he stepped around the table and walked past her. She listened to the echo of his boots as he went upstairs.

She felt rooted in place for several seconds, twisting her dinner napkin back and forth in her hands. The attraction she felt toward him was undeniable. And even hours later, she could still remember the taste of his lips on hers. A slight tremor went through her at the memory. It had been a long time for her as well. And he was her husband...

He was sitting on the bed in the first bedroom. There was a large bay window to the left with a window seat. The setting sun painted the room a dusty rose color.

"I don't sleep in the master bedroom," he explained. He watched her as she scanned the bedroom, taking it all in.

"Why?" she asked softly.

"It's not mine. Never was, and I don't see how it could ever be. Is that a problem?"

She shook her head no. She was still standing in the doorway, and they watched each other across the room. She could see his chest rise and fall with each breath. He seemed to be tracing her whole body with his eyes.

"Come to bed," he told her. His voice was a husky whisper.

Again, a tremor went through her. She felt an ache and longing deep inside. She had not just been alone; she had been lonely. And she had been that way long before Nick got arrested.

"Colt." She came to him, straddling his waist and pushing him down on the bed. She leaned over, creating a canopy with her hair. It blocked out the world, so all that was left was the two of them. They held on to each other. Some moments thrashing against the night and all the loneliness that had held them captive. They were iron and lace, colliding in moments of raw, insatiable need. And in other moments, they were soft and gentle and warm like a summer breeze. Their bodies lifting and swaying like waves to the shore.

PART TWO

Joelle rolled over in bed, pulling the covers around her. She opened her eyes to see that the sun was making its way across the sky. She sighed happily. Her whole body felt sated and relaxed. She smiled, thinking of the night before. She could feel her insides vibrate and stir. She wasn't sure any man had ever made her feel that way. She was literally humming from the inside out. She was more than satisfied, yet the hunger for him lingered.

"Jo."

She jumped slightly, then turned back over in bed. Colt was standing over her, completely dressed. He was clean shaven and he smelled wonderful. She reached out, her hand caressing his.

"Come back to bed," she told him.

"Back to bed?" he repeated. "You need to get up."

She blinked and sat up. She wasn't dressed, so she pulled the sheet up around her.

"What's wrong?"

"There's no breakfast made. And I am heading out. There is housework to be done. I thought we discussed all this."

"Colt..."

"I need a partner, Jo."

"I know that." She blinked several more times, pushing back tears that suddenly burned her eyes. "We were partners last night," she said softly.

"I have to start my day. I'll eat some biscuits left over from last night. But I'll be back at noon, and I'd like something hot waiting for me." He turned then and stalked out of the bedroom.

She smacks away a few tears that had managed to escape. She got out of bed, pulling the sheet along with her. She needed a shower and she needed coffee. And she needed to get herself in check. She couldn't lay in bed daydreaming about him all day. He was a business decision, nothing more.

She padded down the hall, the floor cold against her bare feet. Her clothes were still in her suitcase which she'd left in the foyer. The house was silent as she made her way carefully down the winding staircase. Just as she reached the landing, the front door swung open.

A man stood there looking like John Wayne come back to life. He was most likely in his forties. But a life working under the sun had leathered his skin, and it made him appear older.

"Well, I beg your pardon," he said. He respectfully glanced away as she clutched the sheet tighter.

"Who are you?" she asked.

"Jeff Loggings, darling," he said. "You must be Joelle."

"Good morning." Minnie came through the door but stopped in her tracks when she saw Joelle. "Goodness, Jeff." She slapped his arm. "We're sorry to barge in, honey. Go on up and get yourself ready. It looks like you had a wonderful wedding night." She gave Joelle a wink, and then pushed Jeff toward the kitchen.

She grabbed her suitcase and ran back up the stairs. She was out of the shower and dressed in ten minutes. As she headed back downstairs, the smell of perked coffee wafting up to her.

"I hope you don't mind, I got things started," Jeff said, nodding toward the coffee pot.

"Not at all. Thank you." He handed her a steaming cup. Minnie was bustling around, going back and forth between the refrigerator and the pantry.

"How are you settling in?" Jeff asked as they sat down at the table.

"Just fine."

"Is that so?" Jeff gave her a look that remaindered her of her father.

"I slept in," she admitted. She glanced at the clock hanging on the wall. It was a quarter after seven.

"Getting up at dawn takes getting used to. You'll get into the swing of it. Minnie, Colt and I have been doing it our whole lives. I wouldn't know how to sleep in even if I could."

"I could teach you," she said with a smile.

He returned it. "Don't let him scare you off," he said a moment later.

"Scare me off?"

"Colt is certainly rough around the edges. But beneath all that there is a heart of gold. He's just been lonely too long. And he feels the weight of the world on his shoulders. When his daddy died, it about did him in. That was all the family he had, and he was just here one day and gone the next. I don't think Colt even realizes how much it affected him. How much it broke his heart."

She took a long sip from her cup. She certainly knew about heartbreak.

"He doesn't scare me a bit," she said. "I'm quite fond of him." She was surprised to hear some truth in her words.

Jeff leaned across the table and said quietly, "I know how you met. Minnie doesn't. God don't tell her! But I know. And I know Colt told you he wasn't looking for love."

"He did. I'm not looking for love either," she confessed.

"Is that so? Now, darling, everyone is looking for love. Surely, you know that."

"I've had love."

"And how did that work out?"

"Lousy," she replied. "So lousy that it turned me off to the prospect altogether."

Jeff laughed. He had a genuine twinkle in his eye. "If I had a nickel for every time someone said those words. For every time I said those words."

"But aren't you and Minnie married?" she asked.

"Yes. Third time for me, though. I was pretty bitter on love, but there it was all these years – right in front of my face." He stood up then, draining the last of his coffee.

"Minnie, I am heading out," he called. She was just coming out of the pantry. She came over and kissed his cheek. "It was nice meeting you, Jo."

"It was very nice to meet you, too," she told him.

"I'll see you soon." He put on his hat and tipped it toward her. Then he headed out the back door.

***

Minnie stayed for a few hours. She started a pot of chili, and she showed her around the house. It was almost noon when she left, promising to be back the next day. Joelle started a load of laundry and put some cornbread in the oven. It was ready twenty minutes later when Colt came in.

"Smells good," he said.

"Wash up," she told him.

She gave her a tired smile, and memories of the night before flooded her again. She felt her cheeks go warm and her body go flush as he brushed past her. He stood at the kitchen sink for several minutes, washing away the morning. When he finally sat back down, she placed a hot bowl of chili in front of him.

"I have to go into town this afternoon," he said. He turned to his chili and downed half the bowl in a matter of seconds.

"Should I come?" she asked.

"No need. I have an appointment at the bank. I'm a little behind on the mortgage."

She looked up at him. "What do you mean?"

"My daddy was a great man, but his finances were a mess when he died. I've been working day and night to get things in order again. But times are hard."

She dropped her spoon into her bowl. Bits of chili splashed across the table. "I don't understand. I thought you owned this ranch."

"The bank owns the ranch, Jo."

"But you said you could take care of a wife." She didn't know why she suddenly felt so panicky, but she did.

"I can. The manager is a buddy of mine. Everything will be alright," he said. "I'm doing my best. I've been running uphill for three years now."

"I don't know what to say." And she didn't.

"Listen, I apologize if what I said made you believe I owned this ranch right out. I don't. But I hope to someday. I can tell you this, I will always take care of you. But this isn't a prison, it's a marriage. You can leave anytime you want if this isn't what you want."

"Do you want me to leave?"

"No – I don't."

"I just – I can't go back." Tears burned her eyes. She couldn't look up at him. But she heard him push his chair back and come around the table.

"Then don't." He reached down and tilted her head back so she was looking at him. Then he bent and kissed her lips, softly at first and then harder. He pulled her up from the chair and against him. She wanted him. Wanted him right then and there.

As if reading her mind, he lifted her up and onto the table. He came down on top of her, the weight of him making her whole body ache with want. She arched into him and he moaned softly, his breath warm against her ear. And when he took her, she clung to him as if she was lost at sea and he was the only thing keeping her from drowning completely.

***

Colt left the bank feeling uneasy. He was almost three months behind on the mortgage. Not to mention the taxes were due. He had one month to catch up on payments or the ranch will be put up for auction. He hadn't a clue how he would manage, but he was certainly going to try. He just had to work harder. He knew how to do that.

He spent the next few weeks doing just that and showing Joelle the ins and outs of ranch life. She was able to help with some of the manual labor, but not much. He was simply stronger and had been doing it his whole life. There was always hay to cut, bale and stack. Always a fence that needed mending or manure to haul. Joelle helped with other things. She worked a lot in the garden and with the animals. She seemed to enjoy the animals more than anything, especially the horses. He liked watching her with them. In fact, over the next few days, he caught himself watching her more and more.

He also liked coming home to her – most days. It had become painfully obvious she had never kept house before. She could cook - sure, but nothing from scratch. And she tried baking but burned practically everything. She told him that she cleaned every day. He was sure she did. But it was more like tidying up here and there. She had yet to give the whole ranch the good scrubbing that it needed. It was gnawing at him. They had fought about it more than once.

"I just don't know what you want from me!" she told him.

"You know exactly what I want, Jo. Come on."

"A housemaid."

"A partner! Don't act like I don't work myself into an early grave. Is it so much to ask to have a clean house and a decent dinner?"

She stormed out of the room. He found her an hour later, listening to music in the living room. It was a slow song, something country and twangy. The sun had gone down, and the living room was in shadows. He held out his hand to her, and she took it. They swayed together to the music.

"I am trying," she said sadly.

"I know." He held her, getting lost in the moment.

They went upstairs a little later. This is what he longed for all day. It didn't matter if they had bickered all day, he couldn't wait to get under the blankets with her each night. She was beautiful and soft. She awakened things in him that had been dormant for too long. In those moments, he could care less if she knew how to bake bread or use a vacuum. He was completely under her spell.

***

Joelle sat drinking her third cup of coffee. It was late in the day. Colt would be home soon. A part of her hummed with the anticipation of seeing him. The other part of her worried. She glanced around the kitchen and dining room, searching for some spot she hadn't dusted or dish she hadn't washed. She knew he was disappointed. She was not a housewife. At least not one that lived up to his standards. But she was trying. She was becoming more and more aware of how hard she was trying. How much she wanted to make him happy. That made her nervous. There were days when all she thought about was the moment he would walk through the door.

"Hey," he came in just then. He looked rugged and handsome, tired from a long day. "Something smells sweet."

"I baked a cheesecake today," she said proudly. "And I didn't burn it."

"I didn't know you had to actually bake a cheesecake."

"Exactly," she replied. They both smiled.

He sat down, mail in his hand. He began to shuffle through it as she got up to make him a sandwich.

"Jo, why would a lawyer be writing to you?" he questioned.

She stopped mid-step and turned back toward him. "What?"

He held up one of the envelopes and gave her a questioning stare. "Well?"

"I don't know," she said. "Let me have it." She snatched it from her hand.

"What's going on?" he asked with a frown.

"I think it's just about some property I use to own," she lied.

He stood up and came toward her. "Then let's open it." His voice had gone cold.

"It's personal."

"You're my wife..."

"Colt, please."

"Is this about us, Joelle? What are you trying to do – what are you after?"

"After?" she repeated. "What does that mean?"

"Just open the envelope!"

"You think I trying to take something from you? After the past four weeks, that's what you think of me?"

"I don't know what to think. Just open it."

She threw the letter at him, hot tears springing up in her eyes. "This has nothing to do with you. It's about me. I was married before, Colt. He was a drunk and an abuser, and he's in prison now. And now you know."

He took a step back as if he'd been punched in the gut. "You were married before?"

"I was. He took everything I had. He gambled it away. He drank it away. He became violet when it all ran out. And he almost killed someone." Tears were streaming down her cheeks now. "I'm sorry I didn't tell you. I should have."

"Then, why didn't you?"

"A lot of reasons. Mostly because I didn't want you to know. I didn't think you'd want me if you knew, and I needed you to want me. And I was embarrassed. I had been such a fool for him. And it's hard to admit our mistakes sometimes..."

"You lied to me."

"I'm sorry."

"So am I." He turned and walked out the back door.

"Colt," she said. The tears were raging now. She sunk down on the kitchen tile and cried her eyes out.

PART THREE

Colt didn't sleep at all that night. He stayed downstairs on the couch. He could hear Jo above him, pacing the floor. He could hear when she cried. He wanted to go to her, but he couldn't. Finally, he got up and got in the shower. Joelle had finally fallen asleep, and he didn't wake her before he left. He drove into town. Ashlyn was coming to meet him.

He sat at a back table of the local diner. He and Ashlyn had come here almost every weekend when they were dating. He thought about how young and free they had been. He was still young, but he didn't feel very free anymore.

"Colt."

He looked up, and there she was. She looked just the same, if not more beautiful. He stood up as she fluttered into his arms. When they sat down, she reached across the table and held his hand.

"I've missed you," she said. "I heard you got married."

"I did," he replied with a sad smile.

"I'm happy for you. I mean that," she told him.

He nodded slowly. "I know you do."

"Do you love her?" she asked.

Did he?

He knew he had been falling for her more every day. It hadn't been his plan. But it had happened just the same.

"Love is hard," he said.

"It's not," she replied. "Not everyone runs from love, Colt. Not everyone is as big a fool as I am." She squeezed his hand and then let it go. She shuffled around in her purse and then pulled out an envelope. She slid it across the table.

"This should take care of things," she told him.

"I'll pay you back, I swear."

"I know," she said softly. "I am just glad I could help. I love that ranch. And your daddy would be real proud of you."

"Would he?"

"Believe me, he would. You've built a nice life for yourself. You should let yourself enjoy it."

He smiled at her across the table. "Maybe you're right. It meant a lot to see you, but I should go." He stood up, sliding the envelope into his pocket. He came to the table, bent down and kissed the top of her head. "Thank you."

She nodded, reaching up and taking his hand one more time. She held it for a moment and then let him go for good.

***

Colt had been gone all day. It was getting late, and Joelle was drained. She had packed a bag, and she planned on leaving in the morning. Her heart restricted at the thought. Despite her best efforts, she was falling for him. But the truth was out now, and he didn't want her anymore.

"Hi." Colt appeared in the doorway. "I want you to take a ride with me."

She didn't question him. She just got up and followed him outside. It was cold, and she shivered slightly. The world was dark, not even the moon was out as they headed for the barn. One of the horses was out, already saddled.

They rode for a long time without speaking. She felt like they were the only people left in the world. And when they reached a meadow, he got down off the horse and brought her with him. They sunk down in the cool grass, under the sable sky and made love. It was slow and sweet and tender. So much so that she felt like her heart might burst.

"Every day for the past month I have asked myself the same two questions," he said, lying beside her.

"And what are they?" she asked.

"What am I doing? What are we doing?"

"Come up with any answers?"

He gave her a sideways smile. "Some. But they terrify me."

"Why?"

"Because I'm falling in love with you. I broke my promise. And you lied."

"I'm sorry."

"I know. And I know why you did it. You deserve better than him. And I'm sorry for what he did to you." He reached over and took her hand.

"I didn't want to fall for you either. But I did. A little more every day. Colt – please understand. I didn't know how kind a man could be. And yes, you want things your way. Your stubborn and a perfectionist. And you work too hard. But you're also loving and compassionate. Strong and supportive." She turned to face him.

"Jo..."

"I fell for you, too." She had come here to escape love. But everything catches up to you eventually. No point is running. And she supposed she always knew deep down it would be a losing battle. The first time she saw him, she knew. The first time he kissed her, she knew. And when they made love...well, she certainly knew then.

"I promise never to keep anything from you again," she said.

"And I promise to take care of you every day of my life."

"And I promise to love you, Colt. And never leave you."

"I promise to love you and worship you." He kissed her softly. "This time, I'll keep my promises."

She smiled against his lips. "So will I."

THE END